キャウ

CLAY HURTUBISE

CAW
ENGLISH / JAPANESE
CLAY HURTUBISE, R.Ph.

Reviews

This book had me all over the place, in a good way. — Addie Verna, 12 years old

---

CAW is awesome, his altercations with others left me wanting more. — Taray, always 29

For a black and white book, it sure was colorful. — Patsy, let's just say older and wiser

レビュー

この本は、良い意味で私をあちこち連れて行ってくれました。ー アディ・ヴァーナ、12歳

レビューは最高。彼と他の人との口論はもっと見たいと思わせるほど。ー タライ、いつも29歳

白黒の本なのに、とてもカラフルだった。ー パツィー、歳を重ねて賢くなったと言っておこう

出版社より：本書はフィクションです。名前、登場人物、場所、出来事は、著者の想像の産物、または架空のものです。実在の出来事、場所、人物（生没者を問わず）との類似点はすべて偶然の一致です。
アメリカ合衆国アリゾナ州プレスコットにて出版
アメリカ合衆国にて印刷
Kristen Corrects, Inc.編集
表紙画像：AdobeStock.com
表紙および本文デザイン：Badgerhound Design
初版発行：2017年

Publisher's note: This is a work of fiction. Names, characters, places, and incidents either are the product of the author's imagination or are used fictitiously. Any resemblance to actual events, locales, or persons, living or dead, is entirely coincidental.
Published in Prescott, Arizona USA
Printed in the United States of America
Edited by Kristen Corrects, Inc.
Translated by: Ryo Saito
Cover image: AdobeStock.com
Cover and interior design: Badgerhound Design
First edition published 2017
Hurtubise, Clay
CAW / Clay Hurtubise
Prescott, AZ

About the Author

To this day he does not feel like he fits in this world. Born and raised in Maine, he attended the University of Wyoming School of Pharmacy, joined the Kappa Sigma fraternity, and fell in love with the west. As a youngster, he was tormented by his siblings, bullied at school, and abused by a priest. He and his partner of nearly 30 years, have formed an unorthodox family. Members aren't afraid to show compassion, have empathy, and be there for each other. This is what resonates through both CAW and the sequel, Feathers,

著者について

彼は今でも、この世界に馴染めていないと感じている。メイン州で生まれ育ち、ワイオミング大学薬学部に進学し、カッパ・シグマ・フラタニティに入会し、西部に恋をした。幼い頃は兄弟姉妹にいじめられ、学校ではいじめられ、牧師からは虐待を受けた。彼と30年近く連れ添ったパートナーは、型破りな家族を築いている。家族のメンバーは、思いやりを示し、共感し、互いに寄り添うことを恐れない。これが『CAW』と続編『フェザーズ』の両方に共通する特徴だ。

About the Book

This is a bi-lingual book, with English on the even numbered pages, and an alternate language on the odd numbered pages. CAW, poisoned before birth, is a deformed raven. His and natural family killed off, he must find his way in the world, learning valuable lessons from an odd bunch of characters. He perseveres and is rewarded in the end.

本について

この本はバイリンガルで、偶数ページは英語、奇数ページは別の言語で書かれています。生まれる前に毒を盛られたキャウは、奇形のカラスです。実の家族も殺され、彼は奇妙な登場人物たちから貴重な教訓を学びながら、この世界で生きていく道を見つけなければなりません。彼は粘り強く努力し、最後には報われます。

献身

オーデュボン協会へ

ドレッドロット氏

美しさは目に見える、
目は澄んでいます。
あなたは富を求め、
しかし、あなたはすべてを破壊します。

それほど昔のことではない。メイン州の暗い森の奥深くにひっそりと佇む、人里離れた村。サニービルは北東部全域、いや、その先まで、世界有数の有機栽培果物と野菜の産地として知られていた。イチゴは大きくジューシー、リンゴはシャキシャキと風味豊か。トマトやカボチャといった定番の野菜は、都会の住人が知らないような風味を持っていた。サニービルは数十軒の小規模農家で構成されており、皆が同じ考えを持っていた。それは、化学肥料も農薬も一切使わないということ。それも、たった一人を除いて。

MR. DREDLOT

Beauty is visible,
The eye is clear.
You seek wealth,
But you destroy everything.

It was not that long ago, in a remote village tucked deep in the dark woods of Maine. Sunnyville was known throughout the Northeast—and, some said, beyond—as home to some of the finest organically grown fruits and vegetables in the world. The strawberries were huge and juicy, the apples were crisp and full of flavor, and the staples, like tomatoes and pumpkins, had flavors most city dwellers never knew existed. Sunnyville was made up of dozens of small, independent farmers who all shared the same idea—to use no artificial fertilizers or pesticides. All, that is, except one.

CAW

美しい村は広大な高原に位置していた。サニービル村は、数マイル南に広がる山の頂上が息を呑むほど平坦な姿を除けば、周囲のほとんどの地域よりも標高が高かった。サニービル周辺の土壌は、黒く肥沃で、独特の温暖さを帯びていた。その奥深くには、滋養豊かな水が満ちた温泉が湯気を立てていた。

絵のように美しい村の端には、地面から湧き出る水が岩で囲まれた大きなプールに流れ込み、住民たちは一年中そこで沐浴を楽しみました。雪が降ると、冷たい雪が泡立つ水の中で溶けていく様子が、温かく心地よく感じられ、最高の気分でした。高齢者やアクティブなアスリートたちは、温かいミネラルウォーターが筋肉痛を和らげてくれるため、このプールを好んで利用しました。時が経つにつれ、このプールの癒しの効能は広く知られるようになり、村には天然温泉と大地の恵みを楽しみたいという人々が絶え間なく訪れるようになりました。

The beautiful village was located on a large plateau. The village of Sunnyville was at a higher altitude than most of the surrounding area - except, of course, for the stunning flat top of the mountain a few miles to the south. The soil around Sunnyville was dark, rich and fertile, with an unusual warmth. Deep below were steaming thermal pools filled with nourishing water.

At the edge of the picturesque village, water bubbled up from the ground into a large pool lined with rocks where residents bathed all year round. Some enjoyed it best when it snowed, feeling warm and cozy as the cold snowflakes fell and melted in the bubbly water. Older people and active athletes preferred the pool because the warm mineral water soothed their aching muscles. Over time, word of the pool's healing properties became known, and the village enjoyed a steady stream of visitors who came to enjoy both the natural spa and the fruits of the earth.

CAW

残念ながら、訪問者全員が心優しい人だったわけではありません。その一人、ドレッドロット氏は、暗く陰鬱な心を持つ男で、考えは利己的で貪欲でした。彼は世間に対しては友好的で慈善的な人物として見せかけていましたが…内面は真のドレッドロット氏でした。サニービルのラベルが付いているものは何でも、明るいサニービル村のロゴが入ったラベルを人々が信頼するため、より高く売れることを彼は知っていました。何度か訪問した後、彼は大切な農場を継ぐ後継者のいない、年老いて疲れ果てた農夫、フィールズ氏の信頼を勝ち取りました。ドレッドロット氏は、フィールズ氏が死ぬまで農場に留まり、ドレッドロット氏は納屋の隣に小さな家を建ててそこに住むことを約束しました。これはフィールズ氏にとって望み以上のものであり、彼はドレッドロット氏のような信頼できる人物に農場を譲る機会を歓迎しました。

残念ながら、訪問者全員が心優しい人だったわけではありません。その一人、ドレッドロット氏は、暗く陰鬱な心を持つ男で、考えは利己的で貪欲でした。彼は世間に対しては友好的で慈善的な人物として見せかけていましたが…内面は真のドレッドロット氏でした。サニービルのラベルが付いているものは何でも、明るいサニービル村のロゴが入ったラベルを人々が信頼するため、より高く売れることを彼は知っていました。何度か訪問した後、彼は大切な農場を継ぐ後継者のいない、年老いて疲れ果てた農夫、フィールズ氏の信頼を勝ち取りました。ドレッドロット氏は、フィールズ氏が死ぬまで農場に留まり、ドレッドロット氏は納屋の隣に小さな家を建ててそこに住むことを約束しました。これはフィールズ氏にとって望み以上のものであり、彼はドレッドロット氏のような信頼できる人物に農場を譲る機会を歓迎しました。

Unfortunately, not all of his visitors had kind hearts. One of them, Mr. Dredlot, was a man with a dark, grim heart, his thoughts selfish and greedy. He had learned to appear as a friendly, charitable man to the world... but inside was the real Mr. Dredlot. He had learned that anything with a Sunnyville label could sell for a higher price because people trusted the label with the cheerful Sunnyville Village logo. After a few visits, he had won the trust of an old, tired farmer, Mr. Fields, who had no heirs to pass on his precious farm. Mr. Dredlot promised him that Mr. Fields could stay on the farm until he died, while Mr. Dredlot would build and remain in a small house next to the barns. This was more than Mr. Fields could have hoped for, and he welcomed the opportunity to pass on his farm to such a reliable man as Mr. Dredlot.

Unfortunately, not all of his visitors had kind hearts. One of them, Mr. Dredlot, was a man with a dark, grim heart, his thoughts selfish and greedy. He had learned to appear as a friendly, charitable man to the world... but inside was the real Mr. Dredlot. He had learned that anything with a Sunnyville label could sell for a higher price because people trusted the label with the cheerful Sunnyville Village logo. After a few visits, he had won the trust of an old, tired farmer, Mr. Fields, who had no heirs to pass on his precious farm. Mr. Dredlot promised him that Mr. Fields could stay on the farm until he died, while Mr. Dredlot would build and remain in a small house next to the barns. This was more than Mr. Fields could have hoped for, and he welcomed the opportunity to pass on his farm to such a reliable man as Mr. Dredlot.

人生の大半を過ごした農場で。村の保安官とドレッドロット氏の前で、医師は未亡人となったフィールズ氏が老衰と失意のあまり亡くなったと告げた。ドレッドロット氏は険しい顔で「ああ、なんと悲しいことでしょう。フィールズ氏はこの土地を愛していましたし、私たちも皆、フィールズ氏を愛していました」と言った。皆が頷き合う中、ドレッドロット氏は笑いをこらえ、薄く不気味な笑みを隠すために顔を背けざるを得なかった。

フィールズ氏の死から2年も経たないうちに、ドレッドロット氏は既に彼の土地を取り囲む3つの農場を買い取っていた。頼れる村人たちは彼を仲間の一人とみなし始めていた。残された農民は、あの厄介な少年マイケルを連れた若い農夫だけだった。ドレッドロット氏にとって、それは時間の問題だった。しかし、もはや問題ではなかった。ドレッドロット氏は邪悪な計画を実行するのに十分な土地を手に入れたのだ。

on the farm he had cared for most of his life. In front of the village sheriff and Mr. Dredlot, the doctor announced that the widowed Mr. Fields had simply died of old age and a broken heart. This caused Mr. Dredlot to say with a grim face, "Oh, how sad. Mr. Fields loved this land, and we all loved Mr. Fields." While everyone nodded in agreement, Mr. Dredlot did his best not to laugh, and had to turn away to hide his thin, sinister smile.

Less than two years had passed since Mr. Fields' death, and Mr. Dreadlot had already bought the three farms that surrounded his property. The trustworthy villagers were beginning to think of him as one of their own. The only farmer left was the young farmer with that annoying boy, Michael. For Mr. Dreadlot, it was only a matter of time. But it didn't matter anymore, for Mr. Dreadlot now had enough land to carry out his evil plan.

有機農業は実際には従来の農業と比べてそれほど費用がかからないが、ドレッドロット氏は地元の人々の経済力を超える強欲なビジョンを抱いていた。重機を駆使し、一つの大きな農場を作りたいと考えていた。過剰な肥料、人工成長ホルモン、そして最も毒性の高い殺虫剤の使用も厭わなかった。2年で、4つの古い独立農場を一つの巨大複合農場へと変貌させた。農薬は乱雑に保管し、水や汚染された流出水についても心配しなかった。金こそが全てであり、そして彼は勝利を収めていた。脆弱な環境が大きな代償を払わせたとはいえ、彼は誰よりも土地から多くの収穫を得ていた。

Organic farming is not actually much more expensive than conventional farming, but Mr. Dreadlot had greedy visions that exceeded the means of the locals. He wanted to create one big farm, using heavy machinery, and he had no problem using extra fertilizers, artificial growth hormones, and the most toxic pesticides. In two years, he had transformed these four old independent farms into one big conglomerate mega-farm. He stored his chemicals in disarray and didn't worry about water or contaminated runoff. Money was the name of the game, and he was winning. He produced more from his land than anyone else, although the fragile surroundings paid a heavy price.

キャウ

黒くて小さい、
彼は毒を食べた、毒はそのまま残った。
わらの上、雲の上のように
彼は鳴きながら飛び去った

動かなかった。音も立てなかった。まるで闇に飲み込まれたかのように、真っ黒だった。まるで活字のように真っ黒だった。長く滑らかな羽毛が、ふわふわの明るい雪にきらめいていた。雪は溶けて姿を現した。棒切れで突くと、あっさりと転がった。死んでいた。きっと死んでしまったのだろう、とミハイルは思ったが、その場を立ち去ろうとしたその時、若鳥は片目を開けた。ミハイルは凍りつき、それからゆっくりと身を乗り出して、かわいそうな鳥の様子を確かめた。

CAW

Black and small,
He ate the poison, it lay in place.
On the straw, as if in the clouds,
He flew away, croaking

It did not move. It did not make a sound. It was so black, as if it had been swallowed by darkness. Black as the type on a page. Its long, smooth feathers shimmered against the bright, fluffy snow, which melted and revealed it. When it was poked with a stick, it simply rolled over. Dead. It must be dead, Mikhail thought, but just as he was about to leave the spot, the young bird opened one eye. Mikhail froze, then slowly leaned over to examine the poor thing.

レベッカの両親は60歳近くになる高齢だった。35年以上前、若く気ままな頃、20エーカーの農場を購入した。マイケルの父親と同じように、両親も農薬を信頼しておらず、両家とも有機栽培の菜園で野菜を育てていた。

レベッカは、ほとんどの人にとって、特に学校の筋肉質な運動部の生徒たちにとっては、ごく普通の女の子に見えた。マイケルにとって、彼女はただただ美しかった。細い鼻も、背が高くて細い脚も、彼には見えなかった。二人が会うと、彼はいつも彼女の茶色い瞳を見つめ、そして赤くなって目をそらした。彼女の瞳の中に、彼は彼女の美しさを見つけた。彼が必要とする以上の美しさを。

レベッカは、ほとんどの人にとって、特に学校の筋肉質な運動部の生徒たちにとっては、ごく普通の女の子に見えた。マイケルにとって、彼女はただただ美しかった。細い鼻も、背が高くて細い脚も、彼には見えなかった。二人が会うと、彼はいつも彼女の茶色い瞳を見つめ、そして赤くなって目をそらした。彼女の瞳の中に、彼は彼女の美しさを見つけた。彼が必要とする以上の美しさを。

Rebecca's parents were almost ancient, almost sixty years old. They had bought the twenty-acre farm more than thirty-five years earlier, when they were young and carefree. Like Michael's father, they did not believe in pesticides, and both families grew organic gardens.

Rebecca seemed like an ordinary girl to most people, certainly to the muscular jocks at her school. To Michael, she was simply beautiful. He didn't see her thin nose or her tall, thin legs. When they met, he always looked into her brown eyes, then blushed and looked away. In her eyes, he found her beauty. More than he would ever need.

Rebecca seemed like an ordinary girl to most people, certainly to the muscular jocks at her school. To Michael, she was simply beautiful. He didn't see her thin nose or her tall, thin legs. When they met, he always looked into her brown eyes, then blushed and looked away. In her eyes, he found her beauty. More than he would ever need.

CAW

ドライチャウダーと親切なスタッフ。ゴルパリアン博士は、病気の動物に点滴で栄養を与えるために、実際に牛乳とプロテインパウダーを混ぜました。彼の父親はマイケルに、古くて汚れた水槽を掃除させ、底に新聞紙を敷かせました。それから、錆びた水槽のライトを掃除して点灯させ、病気の動物に少しでも暖かさを届けようとしました。

ミハイルの父親は優しく鳥を調べたが、傷は見つからなかった。鳥は明らかに奇形をしており、ミハイルの父親はそれが若いワタリガラスだと判断するのにしばらく時間がかかった。ミハイルは農場に来るワタリガラスが大好きだったが、ここ1年ほど見かけることが減っていることに気づいていた。最後にワタリガラスが頭上を飛んでいるのを見たのはいつだったかさえ思い出せないほどだった。ワタリガラスは眠らされ、ミハイルと父親にできることはただ待つことだけだった。

ミハイルはカラス科の大きな黒い鳥であるカラスに魅了され、学校の図書館でカラスについて研究しました。

dry chowder and a nice staff. Dr. Golparian actually mixed milk and protein powder to feed the sick creature with an IV. His father had Michael clean out an old, dirty fish tank and line the bottom with newspaper. Then they cleaned and turned on the rusty tank light to shed some warmth on the sick animal.

Mikhail's father examined the bird tenderly and found no wounds. The bird was clearly deformed, and it took Mikhail's father a while to determine that it was a young raven. Mikhail had always loved the ravens that visited their farm, and had noticed over the past year that he had been seeing them less and less. Hell, he couldn't remember the last time he had seen one fly overhead. Now that the bird was put to sleep, all Mikhail and his father could do was wait.

Mikhail was fascinated by crows, a large black bird from the crow family. He studied them in the school library

そして、ワタリガラスは知能が高いことで知られ、体長は最大 27 インチ、体重は最大 3.6 ポンドにまで成長することを知りました。通常は 15 年まで生きますが、40 年まで生きるものも記録されています。ワタリガラスは、カラスとは異なり、くちばしが重く、喉には毛が生えており、ややみすぼらしい外見をしています。ワタリガラスはほとんどどのような環境でも生息でき、エベレストの高度 20,600 フィートでも目撃されています。ワタリガラスはほとんどの子供のように好き嫌いがなく、生きるためならほとんど何でも食べます。また、子供とは違い、幅広い鳴き声があり、周囲の音や人間の話し言葉を真似ることができます。子供のようにいたずらをするのが好きで、缶の蓋をそりにして雪の丘をそりで滑り降りているのが観察されたこともあります。かなりアクロバティックなパフォーマンスを見せることもあり、ループを描いて飛行中に爪を絡ませているのが目撃されています。ある文化ではカラスは悪魔とみなされますが、他の文化ではこの賢い鳥は神に近い存在だと考えられています。

and learned that they are known for their intelligence and can grow up to 27 inches long and weigh up to 3.6 pounds. Although they typically live up to fifteen years, some have been recorded as being up to forty. Unlike crows, ravens have a heavier bill and a furry throat, and are a bit scruffy in appearance. Ravens can live in almost any environment and have been spotted at altitudes of up to 20,600 feet on Everest! These birds are not picky eaters like most children, and will eat almost anything to survive. Also, unlike children, they have a wide range of calls and can mimic sounds made by their surroundings and human speech. Like children, they enjoy playing pranks and have even been observed sledding down snowy hills using can lids as sleds. They can put on quite an acrobatic display - they have been seen intertwining their talons while flying in loops. Although some cultures demonize ravens, others consider this intelligent bird almost divine.

CAW

翌朝、小さなカラスは相変わらず具合が悪く、マイケルの父親は、この苦しみから解放してあげようかと考えました。マイケルは諦めずに頑張ってほしいと懇願し、父親は週末まで鳥を待たせました。そして、運命の最終日まで、毎日同じことが繰り返されました。マイケルと父親は、小さな鳥を苦しめるために納屋へ行きました。水槽に行こうとライトを外したマイケルは、鳥が浮き上がり、そして落ちていくのを見て驚きました。父親は首を横に振り、「わかった。彼が良くなるまで、いくらでも時間をあげよう」と言いました。

赤ちゃんが回復するだろうと確信したマイケルは、梁の上に台を作りました。小枝と葉っぱで粗末な巣を作りましたが、それを見たレベッカは「風で飛ばされた枝の山みたい」と表現しました。その山、いや、巣の隣には窓があり、鳥は

The next morning the little crow was just as sick and Michael's father thought that perhaps they should put him out of his misery. Michael begged them to keep trying and so his father gave the bird until the end of the week. Day after day the same story repeated itself until the fateful last day. Michael and his father went out into the barn to put the little bird out of its misery. When Michael removed the light to reach the aquarium, he was astonished to see the bird rise and then fall. Michael's father shook his head and said, "Okay, we'll give him as much time as it takes to get better."

Knowing the baby would recover, Michael went and made a platform on the beam. He made a crude nest out of twigs and leaves, though when Rebecca saw it, she described it as, "It looks more like a pile of branches blown away by the wind." There was a window next to the pile, er, nest, so the bird could

すべてを見渡せるのに、納屋の好奇心旺盛な猫たちの手が届かない安全な場所にいる。ミハイルは数週間にわたって、1日に2回、梁に登り、改善の兆しを見せ始めた小さな黒い鳥に餌を与えた。時間があれば、ミハイルは鳥を肩に乗せて、用事を済ませながら一緒に歩き回った。鳥は乗り心地を楽しんでいるようで、時折、大きな頭をミハイルの頬にこすりつけていたが、そのせいで頭の大きな鳥が落ちてしまうこともよくあった。

すべてを見渡せる一方で、納屋の好奇心旺盛な猫たちの手が届かない安全な場所にいると感じていた。ミハイルは数週間にわたって、1日に2回、梁に登り、改善の兆しを見せ始めた小さな黒い鳥に餌を与えていた。時間があれば、ミハイルは鳥を肩に乗せて、用事を済ませながら一緒に歩き回った。鳥は乗り心地を楽しんでいるようで、時折、大きな頭をミハイルの頬にこすりつけていたが、そのせいで大きな頭の鳥が落ちてしまうこともよくあった。数週間後、マイケルは再びレベッカを訪ねた。手作りのチョコチップクッキーと新鮮な牛乳を楽しんだ後、レベッカとマイケルは農場を探検しに行った。奇妙な匂いのする小さな川に出会った。二人とも好奇心旺盛だったので、さらに探検してみることにした。その汚らしい川は、マイケルの家族の農場の向こう側の未舗装道路までずっと流れていた。二人は狭い道を渡り、

see everything, but feel safe and out of reach of the curious cats in the barn. Twice a day, for weeks, Mikhail would climb up onto the beam and feed the small black bird, which was beginning to show improvement. If he had time, Mikhail would put the bird on his shoulder and carry it around with him while he went about his duties. The bird seemed to enjoy the rides, occasionally rubbing its huge head against Mikhail's cheek, though this often resulted in the large-headed bird falling off.

A few weeks later, Michael went to visit Rebecca again. After enjoying homemade chocolate chip cookies and fresh milk, Rebecca and Michael went to explore their farms. They came across a small river that had a strange smell. Since they were both inquisitive, they decided to explore further. The nasty river ran all the way to a dirt road on the far side of Michael's family's farm. They crossed the narrow road,

小川を見つけ、次の農場までたどりました。ドレッドロットの農場は完全に柵で囲まれていましたが、レベッカとミハイルは入り方を知っていました。すぐに小川の始まりを見つけました。それはドレッドロットの農場の端にある小さな池でした。本当にひどい臭いでした！レベッカはミハイルに言いました。「一週間クローゼットにしまってあったスニーカーよりも臭いわよ。」

池の横には、フィールズ氏が建てたトタン屋根の古い小屋があった。その蒸し暑い小屋に忍び込んだマイケルとレベッカは、山積みになった農薬の袋を見つけた。中には完全に空っぽの袋もあったが、中には破れて農薬が撒き散らされているものもあった。捕まるのを恐れ、二人は急いで家に戻った。

レベッカの注意深い目が最初にそれに気づいた。カラスの群れが巣を作った下の段には、骨や羽が散らばっていた。雪を押しのけて、マイケルは

found a stream and followed it to the next farm. Dredlot's farm was completely fenced in, but Rebecca and Mikhail knew how to get in. They soon found the beginning of the stream - it was a small pond near the edge of Dredlot's farm. It really stunk! Rebecca said to Mikhail, "It smells worse than your sneakers after they've been in the closet all week."

Next to the pond stood an old shed with a tin roof that Mr. Fields had built. After sneaking into the stuffy shed, Michael and Rebecca found a pile of bags of pesticides. Some of the bags were completely empty, while others had been torn open and were spreading the chemicals around. Not wanting to get caught, they hurried back home.

Rebecca's watchful eyes were the first to notice it. Bones and feathers were scattered around the lower tier where a flock of crows had built their nest. Pushing aside the snow, Michael discovered

何十羽ものカラスの死骸。怖くなった彼らは、急いでマイケル神父のところへ戻りました。発見したことを伝えると、神父はドレッドロット氏の敷地の端まで連れて行ってくれるよう頼み、それから家に帰るように言いました。

ミハイルの父親は、自分の農場とドレッドロット氏の農場の境界線に沿って歩いていた。そよ風がドレッドロット氏の納屋から漂ってくる独特の匂いを運んできた。「農薬の匂いだ」とミハイルの父親は思った。これはただ数羽の鳥が死んだというだけのことではない、もっと複雑な問題だと彼は感じた。彼は調査を続け、ドレッドロット氏に声をかけたが、返事はなかった。

約1時間後、彼は家に戻り、ドレッドロット氏に電話をかけた。ドレッドロット氏は、もし二度と自分の土地に入ろうとしたら、彼と子供たちを不法侵入で訴えると脅した。農場で毒を使ったことは否定も肯定もせず、騒々しい鳥の群れも気にしていなかった。

dozens of dead crows. Now frightened, they hurried back to Father Michael. After they told him of their discovery, he asked them to take him to the edge of Mr. Dreadlot's property, and then told them to go home.

Mikhail's father walked along the border between his farm and Mr. Dreadlot's farm. A light breeze carried a peculiar smell that was coming from Mr. Dreadlot's barn. "It smells like pesticides," Mikhail's father thought. He sensed that the matter was more complicated than just a few dead birds. He continued to investigate and even called out to Mr. Dreadlot, but there was no response.

About an hour later, he returned home and called Mr. Dredlot. Mr. Dredlot threatened to sue him and the children for trespassing if they ever tried to get onto his land again. He neither denied nor confirmed that he used poison on his farm, and besides, he didn't care about the noisy flock of birds.

レベッカの両親は、農薬が害をもたらすどころか害を及ぼしていることを知って、動揺しました。地元の新聞社に連絡しましたが、編集者はドレッドロット氏の親友だったため、記事は掲載されませんでした。郡保安官は、農薬には反対だが違法ではないため、どうすることもできないと言いました。そこでメイン州環境保護局（DEP）に連絡しましたが、彼らは忙しく、メイン州北部の深い森の奥深くにある小さな小川を調べる時間はありませんでした。

春が近づくにつれ、ミハイルのあのおかしなカラスは飛び立たざるを得なくなっていた。ある暖かく晴れた春の日、ミハイルとレベッカが野原を歩いていると、すっかり元気になり、すっかり回復したカラスはミハイルの肩に静かに止まっていた。ミハイルが最初にカラスを見つけた場所に着くと、二人は立ち止まった。カラスはミハイルを見つめ、鼻先を彼の頬にこすりつけた。

Rebecca's parents were upset to hear about the pesticides, knowing that they were doing more harm than good. They called the local newspaper, but the editor was a close friend of Mr. Dreadlot's, and no article was ever published. The county sheriff said that while he was against pesticides, they were not illegal, and there was nothing he could do. They then contacted the Maine Department of Environmental Protection (DEP), but they were too busy to check a small creek deep in the dense forests of northern Maine.

As spring approached, it became obvious that Mikhail's funny raven would have to fly away. Now plump and fully recovered, the raven sat quietly on Mikhail's shoulder one warm, sunny spring day as he and Rebecca walked through a field. When they reached the spot where Mikhail had first found the raven, they stopped. The raven looked at Mikhail, then rubbed its muzzle against his cheek.

そして軽く鼻をくすぐった。ミハイルが答える前に、カラスは飛び立った。ミハイルはすぐに、この飛び方が他の飛び方と違うことに気づいた。まず、カラスは彼らの上空高く舞い上がり、それから急降下して翼を傾け、飛び立ったのだ。

カラスは視界から消える前に、もう一度振り返り、「カーカー」と大きな声で鳴いた。これがカラスが初めて出した音だった。ミハイルは頭を上げてカラスに叫んだ。「カーカー、気をつけて、会いに来て！」

and lightly tickled his nose. Before Mikhail could answer, the raven took off. Mikhail immediately realized that this flight was different from all the others. First, the bird rose high above them, then descended close, tilted its wings and took off.

Before disappearing from sight, the raven turned back once more and cried out loudly, "CAW." This was the first sound it made. Mikhail raised his head and shouted at the bird, "CAW, take care of yourself and come visit!"

カーウとクリスピークルトン

お皿の上には、
運命はあなたの手の中に。
食べ過ぎて、
あなたは死んでしまいます。

CAWがミハイルと父親のもとから飛び立った後、彼がまずしたのは家族を探すことでした。KARは飛ぶのが得意ではありませんでした。理由はいくつかあります。まず、これまで一度も飛んだことがありませんでした。また、両親は毒餌で体を弱らせてしまい、彼に飛ぶことを教えることができませんでした。そして、そして最も重要なのは、KARの頭が大きすぎたことです。実際、KARはほとんど頭だけでした！飛ぼうとすると、いつも頭が地面についてしまいます。地面を見ていると、木や電柱、他の鳥にぶつかってしまうことがよくありました。彼の翼は、可愛らしい巻き毛で飾られていました。

On the plate,
Fate in your hands.
Eat too much,
you'll die.

After CAW flew away from Mikhail and his father, the first thing he did was to look for his family. KAR was not a strong flyer for several reasons. First, he had never really flown before. Also, his parents were too weak from the poisoned food to teach him. Also, and most importantly, KAR had too big a head. In fact, KAR was almost all head! When he tried to fly, his head always went to the ground. Looking at the ground meant that he often flew into trees, telephone poles, and other birds. His wings, adorned with cute curly

羽は短いだけでなく、CAWを変形させた毒によって弱っていました。CAWはこれまで見たことのないようなカラスでした。

キャウにとっては眠ることさえ困難でした。巣の縁に頭を置くと、その重みで押し出されてしまい、「キャーーー！」と叫び続け、ついには地面に落ちてしまうのです。

キャウは短い飛行の後、立ち止まって休憩していました。巨大なオレンジ色の猫に追いかけられた後、CAWは木の上で休憩することを学びました。KARは、休憩する場所に注意するという貴重な教訓を学びました。

カラスは、たとえ奇形のCAWであっても、優れた家系図を持ち、たいていは賢い。CAWは頭が良かった。そこでKARは、最後に両親を見た場所へと向かった。

feathers, were not only short, but also weakened by the poison that had deformed CAW. CAW was a raven such as had never been seen before.

Even sleeping was difficult for CAW. If he laid his head on the edge of the nest, the weight of his head would sometimes push him out and he would scream "CAAAAW!" until he fell to the ground.

CAW would take a short flight, then stop and rest. After being chased by a huge orange cat, CAW learned to take breaks to rest in trees. KAR learned a valuable lesson about being careful where you choose to rest!

Crows, even poor deformed CAW, have strong house abilities and are usually smart. CAW had a lot of brains. So KAR headed to where he last saw his parents

CAW

兄弟姉妹たちもいました。マイケルの家からそれほど遠くなく、彼は日が暮れる頃には昔の巣を見つけました。

空っぽの巣がこんなにたくさんあるなんて、不思議だ、と彼は思った。木から木へと飛び移り、かつての自分の家だと思った場所を見つけた。その日の疲れで、彼はすぐにぐっすりと眠りに落ちた。

カーカーは美しい夢を見ていた。家族と共にふわふわの雲の中を舞い上がり、他のカラスの群れと共に、まるで普通の飛行機のように輪を描いて飛んでいく。ただ、煙の跡の代わりに、時々…えーと…何か余分な荷物が出てくる。爪を握りしめ、一羽は逆さまに、もう一羽は上向きに、そして素早く一回転して舞い上がる。優雅な翼の下に暖かい上昇気流が集まり、カラスはどんどん高く舞い上がり、木々や家々がミニチュアのように見えた。カラスは目を覚ましていた。

and brothers and sisters. It was not far from Michael's house, and he found his old nests by nightfall.

It was strange, he thought, there were so many empty nests to choose from. He flew from tree to tree and found what he thought was his old home. Tired from the day, he soon fell fast asleep.

CAW had beautiful dreams. Soaring through the fluffy clouds with his family, he and a group of other crows flew in rings like regular airplanes — except that instead of a smoke trail, there was... er... some extra baggage that occasionally came out. Clasping their talons, they flew together, one upside down, the other up; then, in one swift motion, they turned over and kept on soaring. Updrafts of warm air gathered under their graceful wings, and they rose higher until all the trees and houses looked like miniatures. They stayed awake.

お腹が空いて楽しい時間が終わったことを思い出すまで、何時間でも簡単に食べ続けることができました。

キャウは早起きが苦手でした。彼は自分をフクロウだと思っていました。いや、夜行性のカラスだと言うべきでしょうか？ヤマネなので、他のカラスが先にミミズを食べてしまうことがよくありました。初めて一人で過ごした日、彼は混乱して目を覚ましました。ミハイルはどこにいる？餌はどこに？それから彼は思い出し始めました。鋭い視力で辺りを見回し、周りに空の巣があることに気づいたのです。巣には彼の嫌いな独特の匂いが漂っていました。しかし、彼は別の匂いも嗅ぎました。小さな池のそばの餌の匂いです。

飛ぶのは彼にとって容易で、ただ滑空して水面に降りていった。辺りを歩き回りながら、様々な食べ物を見つけ、軽く食べた。大きな頭の中で何かが彼を吐き出させ、実際に吐き出した。食べ物を落とし、彼は巣に戻って考えを巡らせた。

for hours on end, easily, until their stomachs reminded them that the fun time was over.

CAW did not like to get up early. He thought of himself as an owl - or should he say a night raven? Since he was a dormouse, other ravens often picked the worms first. On his first day alone, he woke up confused. Where was Mikhail? Where was the food? Then he began to remember. He looked around with his keen eyesight and noticed an empty nest around him. The nest had a particular smell that he did not like. But he also smelled something else - the smell of food near a small pond.

Flying was easy for him, he simply glided down to the water. As he wandered around, he found all sorts of food and ate a quick snack. Something in his big head made him spit it out, and he did. Dropping the food, he flew back to the nest to think things over.

同類の姿が脳裏をよぎった。兄弟姉妹が病気だったことを思い出した。食べ物に毒が入っているとは知らずに、どんどん食べ続ける両親 — それがすべてだった。カー は、飛べなくなった両親が、何かおかしいから家を出るように言ったことを思い出した。ガラスの巣の中で目を覚ましたけれど、少年の腕から逃げるには疲れすぎていたことを思い出した。ミハイル！彼を救ったのはミハイルだった。最初は、KAR は受け入れるのが難しかった。両親からいつも、見知らぬ生き物に近づかないようにと警告されていたからだ。今では、ミハイルと過ごした時間に意味があったが、カーは自分が伴侶なしに生きる運命ではないことを知っていた。

まず、CAWは別の空巣へと飛び立った。巣には昔の仲間たちの匂いがまだ残っていたが、同時に池特有の匂いも漂っていた。下を見ると、もう一羽のカラスがいるような気がした。もしかしたら彼かもしれない。

彼はすぐに滑り降りて隣に着地した

Images of his kind flashed through his mind. Now he remembered his brothers and sisters being sick. His parents eating more and more, not knowing that the food was poisoned—that was it. Now KAR remembered his parents, no longer able to fly, telling him to leave their home because something was wrong. Now he remembered waking up in a glass nest, but too tired to try to escape the boy's arms. Mikhail! It was Mikhail who had saved him. At first, KAR had found it hard to accept, because his parents had always warned him to stay away from strange creatures. Now, the time spent with Mikhail had made sense, but KAR knew that he was not destined to live without a mate.

First, CAW flew to another empty nest. The nest still held the scents of his old friends, but at the same time it emanated the specific smell of the pond. Looking down, he thought he saw another raven. Could it be him?

He quickly slid down and landed next to

動かない鳥。死んでいた。彼の周りには、親戚の死体が横たわっていた。姉妹や兄弟までもがそこにいた。猫も犬もコヨーテも、鳥たちを食べなかった。なぜなら、それらの動物たちは毒を察知して近寄らなかったからだ。

そして、家族の大きな巣がある高い木に着くと、彼は彼らを見つけました。お母さんとお父さん。毒で死んでいました。

キャウは家族と別れなければならないことを分かっていたが、小さな心は粉々に砕け散っていくようだった。キャウは、二度と家族と白い雲の中を飛ぶことはできないと悟った。

小さなお腹がゴロゴロ鳴り始めたので、キャウは食べ物を探しに行きました。ミミズは珍しいようだったので、キャウは飛んで何か美味しいものを探そうと決めました。木の枝に登ってしばらく休みました。時には10分か15分ほど飛んで、止まらざるを得ませんでした。最高の飛行時間でさえ、短いものでした。

motionless bird. Dead. Around him lay the dead members of his extended family. Even his sisters and brothers were there. The cats didn't eat them, nor did the dogs or the coyotes, because all those animals could sense the poison and stayed away.

Then, when he came to a tall tree where his family's big nest was, he found them. Mom and Dad. Dead from poison.

CAW knew he had to leave them, but his little heart felt like it was breaking into tiny pieces. KAR realized he would never fly into the white clouds with his family again.

His little tummy started to rumble, so KAR went looking for food. Worms seemed rare, so KAR decided he would fly and find something else tasty. He climbed up onto a tree branch and rested for a while. Sometimes he could fly for ten or fifteen minutes before he had to stop. Even his best flights were short.

健康で毒を盛られていないカラスと比べると。

キャウは全力を尽くし、正午には良い香りが漂う小さな建物の裏にいた。建物の前には、見えない壁を持つ奇妙で硬い物体がいくつも立っていた。ミハイルはそれを機械と呼んだ。キャウは多くの人がこれらの物体に乗り込んでいるのに気づき、群衆は皆走り去った。しかし、その重い怪物は飽きて止まり、ミハイルのような人々を放り出した。

ここには毒の悪臭はなかった。キャウは建物の裏にある大きな緑色の容器に腰を下ろした。その上に、珍味らしきものが置いてあった。それはまた別の目に見えない物質で覆われていたが、キャウはそれをあっという間に噛み砕いた。ご褒美として、目の前に皿が広げられた。ああ、虫なんていらない、とキャウは思った。食べ物は硬くて、カリカリしていて、それでいて軽かった。

compared to healthy, unpoisoned crows.

CAW did his best, and by midday he found himself behind a small building that smelled wonderful. Many strange, hard things with invisible walls stood in front of the building. Mikhail called them machines. KAR noticed that many people got into these things, then the whole crowd drove away before the heavy beast got tired of it all and stopped, then threw out people like Mikhail.

There was no foul smell of poison here. CAW lowered himself to the large green containers behind the building. There, right on top, was something that looked like a delicacy. They were covered in another invisible material, but CAW quickly gnawed the strange material to shreds. His reward was a plate spread out before him. Ah, who needs worms, CAW thought. The food was hard, crunchy, and light at the same time.

柔らかく淡いベージュ色の角切りの食べ物に、様々な植物の香りが混ざり合った。彼はまず一つだけ慎重に口に運んだ。食べ物はサクサクと音を立て、簡単に小さくて美味しい破片に砕けた。

ああ、なんてことだ、とキャウは思った。これは美味しい！食べ過ぎてはいけないことは分かっていたが、もう1切れくらいなら大丈夫だろう。もう1切れ。もう1切れ。そして、もう残っていなかった。

キャウはひどく喉が渇いたので、水を探しに行きました。これは全く難しくありませんでした。建物の裏からとても硬い枝が出てきていて、そこから水が絶えず滴っていたからです。キャウはその奇妙な枝の下に座り、頭を上に傾けてくちばしを開けました。ポタポタ、ポタポタと水が流れ込み、クルトンがたっぷり詰まったKARのお腹にまっすぐ流れ込んできました。ああ、なんて美味しいんでしょう！

日が沈みかけ、キャウはそろそろ寝る場所を探さなければならないと思った。しかし、一つ問題があった。お腹がいっぱいだったのだ。

The aromas of different plants mingled with the cubes of soft, light beige food. He carefully tried just one at first. The food crunched, easily breaking into small, tasty pieces.

Oh, my God, CAW thought, this is delicious! He knew he shouldn't overeat, but one more piece probably wouldn't hurt. One more. One more. And then there were no more.

Now CAW was incredibly thirsty, and he went to look for water. This was not at all difficult, for a very hard branch came out of the back of the building, and water was dripping from it continually. KAR sat down under the strange branch, tilted his head upward, and opened his beak. Drip, drip, drip the water came—straight into KAR's belly, full of croutons. Oh, how good!

The sun was setting and CAW thought it was time to find a place to sleep. But there was one problem: his belly was so full

重くて飛べませんでした。小さな羽を羽ばたかせながら走り続けましたが、地面から浮かび上がることすらできませんでした。

新たな問題が起きた。夕食が膨らんでいたのだ！クルトンはお腹の中の水で膨らんでいて、食べ物は上がるしかなかった。しまった、これはまずい、とカーカーは思った。それから夕食のほとんどを吐き出したが、今度は吐き気がした。食べ物に毒が混じっているのだろうか？いや、大きな頭は食べ過ぎないようにと訴えていたのに、くちばしが言うことを聞かなかったのだ。今、彼は食べ過ぎの代償を払っている。飛べない上に気分も悪く、安全な隠れ場所を探さなければならなかった。

新たな問題が起きた。夕食が膨らんでいたのだ！クルトンはお腹の中の水で膨らんでいて、食べ物は上がるしかなかった。しまった、これはまずい、とカーカーは思った。それから夕食のほとんどを吐き出したが、今度は吐き気がした。食べ物に毒が混じっているのだろうか？いや、大きな頭は食べ過ぎないようにと訴えていたのに、くちばしが言うことを聞かなかったのだ。今、彼は食べ過ぎの代償を払っている。飛べない上に気分も悪く、安全な隠れ場所を探さなければならなかった。

and heavy, that he could not fly. He ran and ran, and flapped his little wings, but did not even rise from the ground.

Now there was a new problem. The dinner was rising! The croutons were swollen with water in his belly, and there was nowhere for the food to go but up. Oops, this was not good at all, thought KAR. Then he spat out most of the dinner, but now he felt sick. Was the food poisoned? No, his big head had been telling him not to overeat, but his beak wouldn't listen. Now he was paying the price for overindulgence. Unable to fly and feeling sick, he needed to find a safe place to hide.

Now there was a new problem. The dinner was rising! The croutons were swollen with water in his belly, and there was nowhere for the food to go but up. Oops, this was not good at all, thought KAR. Then he spat out most of the dinner, but now he felt sick. Was the food poisoned? No, his big head had been telling him not to overeat, but his beak wouldn't listen. Now he was paying the price for overindulgence. Unable to fly and feeling sick, he needed to find a safe place to hide.

土と、あの大きくて赤い、柔らかいベリーの匂いがした。彼は精一杯中に乗り込み、尾羽が建物に擦れるのを感じるまで後ずさりした。

カーカーにとって、それは長い夜だった。周囲に様々な音が響いていた。ドアの音、人々の叫び声、人が入った奇妙な容器が行き交う音。時折、重々しい足音が近づいてきては止み、そして頭上の容器に何か美味しいものが落とされる音とともに、ゴロゴロと音を立て始めた。やがて彼は深い眠りに落ち、小さなお腹が夕食の残りを片付けた。

キャウは途方もなく大きな音で目を覚ました。彼はそれを見てはいなかったが、大きな緑色のコンテナが頭上高く舞い上がっていた。隣から人の声が聞こえ、そして彼の仮住まいが地面から持ち上げられ、大きなオープンカーに向かって飛んできた。住まいが投げ飛ばされた瞬間、彼は落下し、本能が飛び去るように告げた。

that smelled of soil and those big, red, soft berries. He climbed in as best he could, then backed away until he felt his tail feathers brush against the building.

It was a long night for KAR, as he was surrounded by sounds. The noise of doors, people shouting; strange containers with people in them, coming and going. Sometimes a heavy stomping would approach him, stop, and then start rumbling as something tasty was dropped into the container above him. Eventually he fell into a deep sleep, his little belly taking care of the remains of his supper.

CAW was awakened by a monstrously loud noise. He didn't see it, but a large green container was rising above him. He heard human voices next to him, and then his temporary home was lifted off the ground and flying toward a large open car. As his home was thrown, he fell, and his instincts told him to fly away.

下の人々は彼に向かって叫び続け、長い手足を上に向けていた。

キャウはこの冒険から教訓を学びました。良いものでも、食べ過ぎは長期的には有害になるということです。次回は、少しだけ食べて、残りは後で食べることにします。

The people below kept shouting at him and pointing their long limbs upward.

CAW learned a lesson from his adventure: too much of a good thing can be harmful in the long run. Next time, he'll only eat a few pieces and save the rest for later.

キャウは混乱を招く

異なる視点、
異なる視点、
内側も同じ、
音を超えた。

最初はキャウは一人でいるのが好きでした。しかし、時が経つにつれ、他のカラスたちとの交流が恋しくなってきました。愛する両親が生きていた頃を思い出し、両親が病気の時でさえ、一緒に過ごせる短い時間を楽しんでいました。カーカーは家族について、そしていつか自分も家族の一員になりたいと考えるようになりました。

カラスの群れはしばしば複数の名前で呼ばれます。カラスの群れを「アウトレイジ（暴動）」と呼ぶ人もいれば、「コングレス（会議）」と呼ぶ人もいます。カーカーはコングレスを探したかったのです。コングレスとアウトレイジはよく混同されます。

CAW IS CONFUSING

Different view,
deceived them.
Inside - the same,
surpassed sound.

At first, CAW enjoyed being alone. However, as time slowly passed, he began to miss the company of other ravens. He remembered when his loving mom and dad were alive. Even when they were sick, he enjoyed the short time he had with them. KAR began to think about families and how he would like to be a part of one someday.

A group of crows is often called by more than one name. Some people call a group of crows an "outrage," while others call it a "congress." KAR wanted to find a congress. People often confuse congress with an outrage,

農場で使用されていた殺虫剤が、その地域のカラスのほとんどを毒殺していたため、コングレスはもちろん、他のカラスさえ一羽も見つけることができませんでした。彼は一人で、どんどん広い円を描いて飛び回り、どんどん遠くへ飛んでいき、やがてかつての住処の匂いも感触も感じられなくなってしまいました。

羽毛に覆われた体に頭がほとんどないKARの成長は遅かった。諦めそうになることもあったが、諦めなかった。カーカーは毎日、毎週、一匹ずつ、一匹ずつ、努力を続けた。ミハイルと別れてから1年が経った頃、彼はあの農場で息子とその父親と一緒に暮らしていた方がよかったのではないかと考えた。農場では十分な食料を与えられ、ミハイルは眺めの良い素敵な巣を作ってくれたのだ。諦めかけていたその時、聞き覚えのある音が聞こえてきた。

「カーカー！」

彼の小さな心は喜びで躍り、その鳴き声がどこから聞こえてくるのか確かめようと耳を澄ませました。「カーカー！カーカー！」

Since the pesticides used on the farm had poisoned most of the crows in the area, he had no luck finding Congress, or even a single other crow. Alone, he began flying in wider and wider circles, farther and farther away, until soon he could not even smell or feel his old home.

Being mostly a head with a feathered body, KAR's progress was slow. Although he sometimes felt like he was going to give up, he didn't. KAR kept at it, day after day, week after week, worm after worm. When a year had passed since he had left Mikhail, he wondered if he should have stayed on that farm with the boy and his father. After all, he had been well fed there, and Mikhail had built him a nice nest with a view. He was about to give up when he heard something familiar.

"Caw!"

His little heart leapt with joy, and he listened carefully to determine where the call was coming from. "Caw! Caw!"

カーカーは大きな跳躍とともに、巨大な樫の木の枝から飛び立ち、呼び声の方へ飛び立った。「カーカー！」と鳴き返した。「カーカー！」彼はかつてないほど力強く飛んだ。小さな翼を羽ばたかせると、家族と小さなカーカーたちの姿が目の前に現れた。間もなく、また「カーカー！」という音が聞こえた。そしてまた！空気は「カーカー！」で満たされた。それは狂気だった！古木の茂る林の中で、大規模な集会が開かれていた。カラスが地平線まで飛んでいく。葉のない木々は、たくさんの鳥たちのせいで、巨大な黒い塊のように見えた。

長い間他のカラスと交流していなかったカーカーは、適切なエチケットを知らなかった。彼はカラスの真ん中に飛び込み、まるで集会で政治家のように話し始めた。KARは他のカラスとは比べ物にならないほど大きな「カーカー」という鳴き声をあげていたが、まさにその最中に撃ち落とされてしまった。

枝から落ちた。「キャーーーーーーーーーーー！」と悲鳴を上げて頭から落ちた。

With a great leap, CAW left his branch high in the mighty oak and flew toward the call. "Caw," he called back, "Caw!" He flew stronger than ever. He flapped his little wings as visions of his family and the little KARs came before his eyes. It wasn't long before he heard another "Caw!" - and another! The air was filled with "Caw!" It was madness! There, in a thick grove of old trees, was a huge convention. Crows to the horizon. The leafless trees looked like a great black mass, for there were so many birds.

Having not interacted with other crows for a long time, KAR did not know proper etiquette. He flew straight into the middle and started talking like a politician at a rally. Right in the middle of one of his loudest "caws", because KAR could caw like no other crow, he was shot down

from the branch. "Caaaaaaaaaaaaaaaaaaaaaaaw!" he squealed, falling head first.

CAW

他のカラスたちは彼を笑った——笑いながらカーカー、カーカーと鳴き続け、笑い続けた。彼が飛び戻ろうとすると、彼らはさらに大きな声で笑い、また彼を撃ち落とした。あるカラスは彼はカラスなんかじゃない、と言い、別のカラスは彼はカラスだけど愚かなカラスだ、と言い、さらに別のカラスは彼は史上最も醜いカラスだと言った。

この出来事は何時間も続いた。キャウは怒りを抑えようとした。なぜこんなことが起きているのか理解しようとした。他のカラスたちは彼が誰なのか全く分からなかった。夕方までに議会は彼に我慢の限界を迎え、カラスであろうとなかろうと、KARは彼を歓迎しないと告げた。

傷心の彼は、視界から消え、夜の間、静かに眠りについた。キャウは、人々が笑い、冗談を言い合う議会の話を聞きながら、空高く舞い上がった。

The other crows laughed at him - laughing and cawing, cawing and laughing. When he tried to fly back, they only laughed louder and shot him down again. One said he was not a crow at all; another said he was a crow, but a stupid one; and yet another said he was the ugliest crow of all time.

This went on for hours. CAW tried not to get angry. He tried to understand why this was happening. To the other crows there was complete confusion about who he was. By evening, Congress had had enough of him and told KAR that, crow or not, he was not welcome.

Broken-hearted, he flew out of sight and settled down for the night. CAW listened to the congress as they laughed and joked with each other. They soared into the air

そして舞い上がり、群れに戻ってきて、カラスにとってなんて素晴らしい日なんだろう、と叫びました。カラスは悲しみに打ちひしがれました。

翌朝、議会の喧騒が耳に響く中、キャウは空へと舞い上がり、飛び去っていった。カラスたちが彼の姿を見て、飛び立つ彼を罵倒した。落胆したキャウは、その日は遠くまで飛ぶ気力もほとんど残っていなかった。議会と共にあの日を生き延びるまでには、数週間かかるだろう。どうして彼らは、自分たちの仲間にあんなに残酷なことをできるのだろう？見た目が違うのは分かっていたが、それがなぜ問題になるのだろうか？

約1ヶ月後、彼はまた別のコンベンションを見つけた。最初のものほど規模は大きくなかった。彼らは彼をせがむどころか、入場は許可してくれたものの、ほとんど無視していた。一人のカラスガールが彼の小さな心をときめかせたが、彼女は彼とは全く関わりたがらなかった。誰も彼に気付いていないようだった。仲間たちの間でも、キャウは孤独だった。

and soared, then rejoined their group and exclaimed what a beautiful day it was to be a raven. Sadness overcame CAW.

The next morning, with the noise of Congress filling his ears, KAR took to the air and flew away. Some of the crows saw him go and called him names as he went. Dejected, he had little strength to fly far that day. It would be weeks before he could live through that day with Congress. How could they be so cruel to one of their own? He knew he looked different, but why should it matter?

About a month later, he found another convention, not as big as the first. Instead of pestering him, they let him in, but mostly ignored him. There was one crow girl who made his little heart flutter with delight, but she wanted nothing to do with him. No one seemed to notice him at all. Even among his fellows, CAW was lonely.

ある朝、キャウは、以前そこにいたのと同じような大きなオレンジ色の猫がカラスを一羽追い払っているのに気づきました。彼は、その大きな猫が大きな家に入れられ、きらきらと輝くガラスのドアの前に立つのを見ていました。キャウは悪意はありませんでしたが、他のカラスたちに良い印象を与えたいと思っていました。国会議員になり、受け入れられたかったのです。そこで、ガラスのドアの前にある木の棒から降りて着地しました。そして、執拗に猫をからかいました。キャウはドアに近づき、猫の目の前でドアをつつき、転がって死んだふりをしました。猫は激怒しました！キャウは後にカラスが彼を「オールドオレンジ」と呼ぶことを知りましたが、彼はカーテンに飛び乗って、紙吹雪のように引き裂きました。時々、オールドオレンジは気絶するためだけにドアに体を投げつけました。そしてそこに座って、声が枯れるまでニャーニャーニャーと鳴きました。若い議員たちは楽しい時間を過ごし、キャップに延々と語りかけました。

One morning he noticed a large orange cat, like the one that had been there before, chase away one of the crows. He watched as the large cat was let into the great house and stood in front of the glittering glass door. CAW had no malice in his soul, but he wanted to impress the other crows, he wanted to be a member of Congress, to be accepted. So he climbed down and landed on a wooden pole in front of the glass door. He teased the cat relentlessly. CAW would walk up to the door and peck at it right in front of the cat, then roll over and play dead. The cat was furious! Old Orange, as CAW later learned the crows called him, would jump on the curtains, tearing them like confetti. Sometimes Old Orange would throw himself at the door, just to stun himself. Then he sat there and meowed, meowed, meowed until his voice broke. The young members of Congress had a great time, encouraging the CAP to go on and on.

これこそが自分が探し求めていたものだと彼は思いました。自分の居場所を見つけたのです。

年老いたカラスがキャウに「立ち止まって枝に一緒に来るように」と呼びかけると、キャウは大喜びしました。自分の家を見つけたと確信し、もうすぐキャウ夫人にも会えるだろうと思いました。年老いたカラスは数分間何も言わず、ようやく口を開くと、キャウになぜあんなことをしたのかと尋ねました。CAWは、以前オールドオレンジがカラスの一羽を追い払ったことを知っていて、キャウはただ猫に仕返しをしただけだと言いました。結局のところ、猫と鳥は仲が悪いのですから。

年老いたカラスはキャウを見て、キャウが困惑していると言った。確かに鳥と猫は必ずしも仲良くできるわけではないが、だからといって猫をいじめる理由にはならない。カラスは猫が好きではないかもしれないが、標的にする必要はない。

それから老いたカラスは数分間沈黙した後、口を開いた。「カー」と彼は言った。「君は確かに辛い人生を送ってきたが、

He thought this was what he had been looking for! He had found his home.

When the older raven called to CAW to stop and join him on the branch, CAW was delighted. He was sure that he had found his home and would soon find Mrs. CAW. The old raven did not speak for several minutes, and when he did, he asked CAW why he had done what he had done. CAW said that he knew that Old Orange had chased away one of the crows earlier, and CAW was simply getting back at the cat - after all, cats and birds do not get along.

The old raven looked at CAW and said that CAW was confused. Yes, birds and cats do not always get along, but that is no reason to tease the cat. Although ravens may not like cats, there is no need to make a target out of them.

Then the old raven was silent for a few minutes before speaking. "KAR," he said, "it's clear you've had a hard life, but

「何も学んでないね。少しからかうのは構わないけど、君のしたことは残酷だ」老いたカラスは、キャウに一人で旅に出て、他の種族や他のカラスに敬意を払うことを学ばせるよう提案した。しばらくすれば、戻ってくるかもしれない。

キャウは驚愕した。他のカラスたちが煽動していたのに、なぜ罰せられなかったのかと。

「カウ」と老いたカラスは言った。「彼らも学ぶだろうが、君はもう十分大人だ。正しい行いの模範を示さなければならない。」

再び、キャウは単独航海に出発した。

"You haven't learned anything. A little teasing is okay, but what you did was cruel." The old raven suggested that KAR go on a solo journey and learn to treat other species and other ravens with respect. Perhaps after some time, he could return.

CAW was stunned. He said that the other crows were egging him on, so why weren't they punished?

"CAW," said the old raven, "they will learn too, but you are old enough to know better. You must set an example of proper behavior."

Once again, CAW set out on a solo voyage.

翌朝、彼は自分でミミズを取りに行き、たっぷり朝食をとった。いつもの場所に戻ると、他のカラスが近づいてくるのに気づいた。そのうちの一羽は美しい雌で、KARの心臓は再び高鳴った。その雌が時折彼の方を見ているのに気づいた。もしカラスが赤面できるなら、彼はまるでカージナルのようだっただろう。

しばらくして、年老いたオスの一羽が、なぜそんなに変な顔をしているのかと尋ねました。キャウは、みんな変に見えたからだと答えました。年老いた鳥はしばらく考えた後、質問を言い換えたいと言いました。

「カァー」と彼女は言った。「あなたたちはみんなカラスなの？もしそうだとしたら、なぜそんな風に見えるの？」

キャウは毒物について、そして彼の家族がどのように亡くなったのかを説明しました。議会全体が彼の話を聞きたがっていました。CAWの話に耳を傾ければ、毒物を避ける方法を学べるからです。彼はその臭いについて説明しました。

The next morning he went to get the worms himself and had a hearty breakfast. When he returned to his old place, he noticed that some other crows had approached him. One of them was a beautiful female, which made his heart beat faster again. KAR saw that she sometimes looked in his direction, and if crows could blush, he would have looked like a cardinal.

After a while, one of the older males asked him why he looked so strange. CAW replied that they all looked strange to him. The old bird thought about it for a while, and then said that she wanted to rephrase the question.

"CAW," she said, "are you all crows, and if so, what makes you look the way you do?"

CAW went on to explain about the poison and how his family had died. The entire congress wanted to hear his story because if they listened to CAW, they could learn to avoid the poison. He explained the smell

できる限りのことをすると、他のカラスの一羽も以前同じ匂いを嗅いだことがあると言いました。カラス保護局はカラスたちに、その匂いに近づかないように、そして食べ物に気をつけるようにと警告しました。

彼が話している間も、メスのカラスはどんどん彼に近づいていきました。ついに二人はすぐ隣り合わせになりました。他のカラスは二人に少し距離を置いてくれました。彼女はキャウに、彼の見た目が好きだと言いました。そしてまた、カラスが赤面できたらいいのに！キャウは彼女の顔に触れようと身をかがめましたが、頭を下げすぎてしまい、「カ————！」と大きな声で叫び、再び地面に倒れてしまいました。硬い地面に頭がぶつかる鈍い音がしました。今度は笑う代わりに、他のカラスは大丈夫かと尋ねました。キャウは慣れていると答えました。枝に戻り、美しいカラスの隣で、キャウは幸せな気持ちになりました… 気持ちが悪かったけれど、とても幸せな気持ちでした。

as best he could, and one of the other crows mentioned that she had smelled the smell before, too. CAW warned them to stay away from it and to be careful what they ate.

All the while he was talking, the female crow was getting closer to him. Finally, they were right next to each other. The other crows gave them some personal space. She told CAW that she liked the way he looked - and again, if only crows could blush! CAW leaned down to touch her face, but he lowered his head too far and let out a loud "Caaaaaaaw!" and fell to the ground again. There was a dull thud as his head hit the hard ground. This time, instead of laughing, the other crows asked if everything was okay, and he told them he was used to it. Back on the branch, next to the beautiful crow, CAW felt happy... sick, but very happy.

キャウの復活

弾丸は恐ろしい。
その少年は死んだ、
再びくちばしが救うだろう、
暗いけれど明るい道。

時が経つにつれ、マイケルとレベッカはより親密になっていきました。レベッカはマイケルが仕事をしている時によく訪ね、お菓子を持ってきてくれました。キャウが飛び去って以来、姿が見えていなかったため、二人はキャウのことなど考えもしませんでした。カラスは、以前の土地が汚染されていることを知っていたので、マイケルとレベッカの農場から遠く離れた場所に巣を作りました。

高校卒業後、ミハイルとレベッカが再び校庭を歩いていると、あの忘れられない叫び声が聞こえた。「カーン！」

The bullets are terrifying,
The boy is dead,
Again the beak will save,
A dark but bright path.

As time passed, Michael and Rebecca grew closer. Rebecca loved to visit Michael when he was working and bring him sweets. They did not think about KAR because they had not seen him since he flew away. The crows moved their nesting grounds far from Michael and Rebecca's farms because they knew their old land was poisoned.

After high school graduation, Mikhail and Rebecca were once again walking across the field when that never forgotten cry was heard. "CAW!"

見上げると、なんと一羽ではなく二羽のカラスが彼らの上に降りてくるのが見えた。カーはミハイルの肩に止まり、カラスの少女カーはレベッカの肩に止まった。

キャウは何分間も歌い続けました。まるでヒバリのように嬉しそうに、「カー、カー、カー！」と歌い続けました。

カウ夫人はレベッカの肩に留まり、レベッカの頬に頭をこすりつけて愛情を示しました。すると、到着した時と同じように、二羽の鳥は飛び立ちました。今度は姿を消すどころか、古い納屋へと向かい、見慣れた古い梁の上に、すぐに立派な巣を作りました。

皆、すっかり落ち着きました。ミハイルはキャウが仲間を連れて戻ってきてくれたことにとても喜んでいました。

時が流れ、再び冬が訪れた。ある日、マイケルは寒くて風の強い日、畑を横切る日課の旅をしていた。

When they looked up, they saw not one, but two crows descending upon them. Kar landed and perched on Mikhail's shoulder, and the crow girl, KAR, perched on Rebecca's shoulder.

CAW couldn't stop singing for several minutes. He was as happy as a lark and kept singing "CAW, CAW, CAW!"

Mrs. CAW simply remained on Rebecca's shoulder and showed her affection by rubbing her head against Rebecca's cheek. Then, as quickly as they had arrived, the two birds took off. This time, instead of disappearing, they headed for the old barn, where they quickly built a proper nest on an old familiar beam.

Everyone settled in well. Mikhail was so happy that CAW had returned and brought his mate with him.

Time passed and winter came again. One day, Michael was making his daily journey across the field in the cold, windy

聞き慣れた狩猟用ライフルの音を聞いた日。この辺りはよく知っていて、鮮やかなオレンジ色の帽子をかぶっていたので、恐怖は感じなかった。クリスマス直前で、少なくとも公式には狩猟シーズンは終わっていた。

次の銃声と、ミハイルの胸に突然襲い掛かる鋭い痛みは、まるで同時に起こったかのようだった。彼は後ろに倒れ、傷口から大量の血を流した。しばらく意識を失い、ひどく寒かった。周囲の真珠のような白い雪はピンク色に染まり、ルビー色の頬はゆっくりと青みがかった白く変色していった。目が覚めると、彼は暖かいベッドに横たわっていた。地元の医者が包帯を巻き終えたばかりだった。

父親のレベッカと彼女の両親は部屋にいて、カメラマンたちは居心地の良いキッチンで待機していた。ミハイルの父親は、ミハイルがどうやって戻ってきたのかを説明した。キャウは何か異変を感じて飛び出した。彼はミハイルの上に座って、ミハイルがどこにいるのかを突き止めた。

the day he heard the familiar sound of a hunting rifle. Familiar with the area and wearing his bright orange cap, he felt no fear. It was just before Christmas and, officially at least, hunting season was over.

The sound of the next shot and the sudden sharp pain in Mikhail's chest seemed to be simultaneous. He fell backwards, bleeding profusely from the wound. He was unconscious for some time and very cold. The pearly white snow around him took on a pink tint, while his ruby cheeks slowly turned a pale white with a hint of blue. When he awoke, he found himself in his warm bed. The local doctor had just finished bandaging him.

His father, Rebecca and her parents were in the room while the photographers waited in the cozy kitchen. Mikhail's father explained to him how he had returned. KAR sensed something was wrong and flew out. He sat on Mikhail and found where the

弾丸はミハイルの心臓に突き刺さっていた。奇妙な形の頭とくちばしのおかげで、彼は傷口を開き、弾丸を取り出すことができた。それから家に戻り、ミハイルの父親が気づくまで台所の窓をノックした。彼はカラスが中に入ってくることを十分に理解しており、そうするとカラスは台所のテーブルに止まり、血まみれの弾丸をバキッと音を立てて押し出した。ミハイルの父親はジャケットを掴んで家から飛び出し、カラスの後を追った。カラスは彼を意識を失ったミハイルのもとへ連れて行った。その後は、言うまでもなく、歴史の続きとなった。

銃弾の追跡先は、有名なドレッドロット氏でした。彼は狩猟免許を取り消されていただけでなく、狩猟シーズン外に狩猟をしていました。保安官は発砲が偶発的なものではなかったと判断し、ドレッドロット氏は郡刑務所に送られました。

ドレッドロット氏が獄中にあった時、彼の生涯を詳細に記した日記が発見された。それは彼が幼い頃から始まっていた。

bullet, close to Mikhail's heart. With the help of his oddly-shaped head and beak, he was able to open the wound and extract the bullet. He then returned home and knocked on the kitchen window until Mikhail's father noticed him. He knew well enough to let CAW in, and when he did, the raven landed on the kitchen table and pushed the bloody bullet out with a crack. Grabbing his jacket, Mikhail's father ran out of the house and followed CAW, who led him to an unconscious Mikhail. After that, as they say, the rest is history.

The bullet was traced to a well-known Mr. Dreadlot, who not only had his hunting license revoked, but was also hunting out of season. The sheriff decided the shooting was not accidental, and Mr. Dreadlot was sent to the county jail.

While Mr. Dreadlot was in prison, journals were found detailing his entire life. They began when he was a small boy,

CAW

そして、彼の同族に対する嫌悪感で満ち溢れていた。彼の最後の日記の一つには、サニービル村を乗っ取る計画、フィールズ氏を巧みに殺害した計画、そして土地を売却したくない農民を追い出すために使う計画が記されていた。殺虫剤が初めて発見された時のミハイルとレベッカとの出来事が日記のかなりの部分を占めていた。ドレッドロット氏はミハイルへの復讐を誓った。殺人については触れられていなかったものの、彼が復讐に反対していないことは明らかだった。日記には、ある凍えるような冬の夜にミハイルの家で悲惨な火事が起こると書かれていた…そして、ドレッドロット氏がどれほど取り乱すかが書かれていた。そして、その後ろには幸せそうな顔が描かれていた。

ドレッドロット氏が刑務所に収監されていた時、納屋に積まれていた化学薬品の山が倒れ、肥料の山と混ざって発熱し始めた。自然発火と呼ばれる現象だが、地元の人々はそれを運命と呼んだ。

その月の後半、マイケルとレベッカは

and were filled with his disgust for his kind. One of his last journals contained his plan to take over the village of Sunnyville, his accomplished murder of Mr. Fields, and the methods he planned to use to drive out farmers who did not want to sell their land. The incident with Mikhail and Rebecca when the pesticides were first discovered occupied a significant portion of the journal. Mr. Dreadlot swore vengeance on Mikhail. Although he did not mention the murder, it was clear that he was not against it. The journal spoke of a tragic fire in Mikhail's house that would occur some freezing winter night... and how upset Mr. Dreadlot would be. This was followed by a happy face: ?.

While he was in jail, a stack of Mr. Dreadlot's chemicals in his barn tipped over. They mixed with a pile of his fertilizer and began to heat up. It's called spontaneous combustion, but the locals called it fate.

Later that month, Michael and Rebecca

子猫たちは納屋に忍び込み、干し草の上に落ち着きました。まさに初めてキスをしようとしたその時、頭上からものすごい音が聞こえ始めました。子猫たちは仰向けになって、その貴重な光景を見上げました。キャウ夫妻は巣の中で誇らしげに、小さなCAWたちの列の前の列に立ち、見下ろしていました。一行は皆で「カーカー、カーカー、カーカー！」と叫びました。

それからキャウは小さな子供たちを前に並べ、キャウ夫人と二人は一団の後ろに立った。キャウは、季節によって人々が好む歌が違うことを知っていた。季節は終わっていたけれど、このプレゼントは最高だった。キャウがくちばしで梁を三回叩くと、一団全員が「ジングルベル」のメロディーに合わせて歌った。

カウ、カウ、カウ

カウ、カウ、カウ

カウ、カウ、カウ、カウ

カウカウ、カウ、カウカウカウ

crept into the barn to settle down in the hay. Just as they were about to kiss for the first time, a tremendous noise began above them. They rolled over on their backs and looked up at the precious sight. CAW and Mrs. CAW stood proudly in their nest in front of the entire line of little CAWs, looking down on them. The whole gang was shouting, "caw-caw, caw-caw, caw-caw!"

Then CAW lined up the little ones in front, and he and Mrs. CAW stood behind the troop. CAW knew that people liked certain songs at certain times of the year. Although the season was over, the present was perfect. CAW tapped his beak three times on the beam, and then the whole gang sang to the tune of "Jingle Bells":

Caw, Caw, Caw

Caw, Caw, Caw

Caw, Caw, Caw, Ca-Caw

Caw Caw, Caw, Ca-Caw-CAW Caw

カァーカァーカァー

ああ…（キャウが完璧に真似した）

カーカー、カーカー、カー

カーカー、カーカー、カー

カーカー、カーカー、カーカー…

すると、ミハイルとレベッカの笑い声で大混乱が巻き起こった。カラスが笑えないと思っているなら、この会議を一度見てみるべきだ！

Caw Caw Ca-Caw Caw

Oh… (CAW mimicked this perfectly)

Caw, Caw, Caw

Caw, Caw, Caw

Caaaaaaaw Caw Caw Caaaaaaaawww…

Then pandemonium broke out among the laughter from Mikhail and Rebecca. And if you thought ravens couldn't smile, you should have seen this congress!

Other books by Clay Hurtubise, R.Ph.

Then I Sold It: A Memoir

An adventurous motorcycle ride that nearly cost him his life, more than once.

While a student at the school of pharmacy at the University of Wyoming, the school sponsored a 'drug trip' to the Midwest to visit pharmaceutical companies. Lacking the funds to go on the trip, he jumped on his Yamaha 650 and headed for the Pacific coast.

On the first day, he drives through a snow squall, is in a traumatic accident, and someone tries to kill him.

Waking up the next morning, he continues his journey thinking, “It must get better,” but does it?

Shaman: Devil's Deal ;

chronicles the life of a young shaman who must learn his powers quickly, as an evil force has invaded his neighborhood. Learning the meaning of family, he finds himself and his new family stronger than he ever imagined.

Feathers

Feathers the sequel to CAW, is also a side-by-side bilingual book. In Feathers, an unlikely group of animals band together. They are an unlikely group: a sheepdog, a fluffy cat, ravens, and a chipmunk. They face multiple threats and must defeat them. Along the way, a misguided little boy is wounded and lost. Will the animals save the boy who tormented them?

Who hasn't had an 'if only' moment? If only I used my original lottery numbers, had approached the cutie at the bar, didn't have that 'one for the road'.

Join Clay as he experienced a multitude of 'if only' events.

Think of your own ‘if only’ moments and how choosing one path led your life down a vastly different path, if only you had chosen the alternative.

The author's first play.

The Watch follows a man obsessed by a passion that, in his mind, will show the world that he 'made it'.

Witty, funny, and sad. This play reinforces the belief that family comes before possessions. It ends with compassion, forgiveness and understanding. Favorite character? The dancing skeleton.

The fascinating and thought-provoking memoir Fred, a Ghost Story by Clay Hurtubise explores the paranormal experiences of a once-skeptical man whose life was irrevocably altered by a string of spectral encounters. The fact that this book is based on actual events and features Clay's candid, unvarnished account of his journey from incredulity to reluctant acceptance distinguishes it from other ghost stories. All events in this book are true and told to the best of the author's recollection.

I love a good ghost story – and I especially love a TRUE ghost story. This is why I was very excited to receive a review copy of this book from an author I have read and enjoyed before. Let me tell you more about it, and why I enjoyed it!

Dedication: "Fred, whom I believe to be Mitchell Allen. One of the gentlest and kind souls to walk this earth."

Fred, a ghost at the center of the narrative, transforms from an unsettling apparition into a protector who even saves Clay and his partner's lives at a crucial juncture. We can almost feel as though we are there with the author as he describes these experiences in exquisite detail, experiencing the unexplainable with him. (Some names have been changed but the story is true.)

But not every interaction in this memoir is positive. The story is made more intimate and eerie by the terrifying appearance of a ghostly priest who mistreated Clay as a youngster. Here, the book goes beyond ghost stories to provide readers with a moving examination of tragedy, memory, and recovery. The narrative is grippingly tense because of the contrast between these two spirits – one a savior, the other a tormentor.

Clay's early reluctance to accept the supernatural is among the most fascinating elements in Fred, a Ghost Story. His early sightings had been dismissed as hallucinations or the product of an overactive imagination due to a head injury. However, Clay is forced to consider the idea that what he is seeing might not be merely his imagination when his dog responds to something invisible. Particularly for readers who might have the same early misgivings as Clay, this slow transition from skepticism to acceptance gives the novel an authentic and relatable feel.

With brief bursts of dry humor interspersed with the more somber subjects, Clay Hurtubise's writing is clear-cut and captivating. His reports gain credence since he vividly describes the ghosts and their interactions without going beyond with sensationalism. Another important character in the narrative is the author's spouse, who provides a helpful viewpoint that counterbalances Clay's struggle with faith.

To sum it up, Fred, a Ghost Story is a profoundly human tale about overcoming anxieties, addressing the past, and seeing meaning in the inexplicable—it is more than just a book about ghosts. With an honest candor, Clay Hurtubise draws readers into his world, making it difficult to put the book down. This memoir will make you wonder about the limits of reality, regardless of your level of faith in the paranormal or your level of skepticism.

To anyone who appreciates emotional memoirs, true-life paranormal events, or stories that go against the grain, I heartily suggest this book!

It's available on Amazon in paperback and Kindle edition, as well as in Kindle Unlimited.

www.ingramcontent.com/pod-product-compliance
Lightning Source LLC
Chambersburg PA
CBHW020629250626
47154CB00004B/1737

* 9 7 8 1 9 3 6 8 7 7 3 3 1 *